ughty book I promise not to be a naughty book I promise
aughty book I promise not to be a naughty book I promise
aughty book I promise not to be a naughty book I promise
aughty book I promise not to be a naughty book I promise
ughty book I promise not to be a naughty book I promis
ughty book I promise not to be a naughty book I promise
aughty book I promise not to be a naughty book I promise
ughty book I promise not to be a naughty book I promise
rughty book I promise not to be a naughty book I promise
aughty book I promise not to be a naughty book I promise
ughty book I promise not to be a naughty book I promise
ughty book I promise not to be a naughty book I promise
ughty book I promise not to be a naughty book I promise
ughty book I promise not to be a naughty book I promise
iughty book I promise not to be a naughty book I promise
ughty book I promise not to be a naughty book I promise
ughty book I promise not to be a naughty book I promise
ughty book I promise not to be a naughty book I promise
ughty book I promise not to be a naughty book I promise

This $\overset{\text{naughty}}{\wedge}$ book belongs to

For Polly and Sheila

Henry Holt and Company, LLC, *Publishers since 1866*
175 Fifth Avenue, New York, New York 10010 [mackids.com]

Henry Holt® is a registered trademark of Henry Holt and Company, LLC.
Copyright © 2014 by Richard Byrne
All rights reserved.

Library of Congress Cataloging-in-Publication Data is available.

ISBN 978-1-62779-071-0

Henry Holt books may be purchased for business or promotional use. For information on
bulk purchases, please contact Macmillan Corporate and Premium Sales Department
at (800) 221-7945 x5442 or by e-mail at specialmarkets@macmillan.com.

First published in hardcover in 2014 by Oxford University Press
First American edition—2014
Printed in China by Leo Paper Group,
Gulao Town, Heshan, Guangdong Province

10 9 8 7 6 5 4 3 2

This book just ate my dog!

Richard BYRNE

WALKIES!

LET'S GO!

Henry Holt and Company
New York

Bella was taking her dog for a stroll across the page when . . .

. . . something
very odd happened.

Bella's dog disappeared.

"Hello, Bella.
What's up?"
said Ben.

"This book just ate my dog!"

Ben decided
to investigate.

But Ben disappeared too.

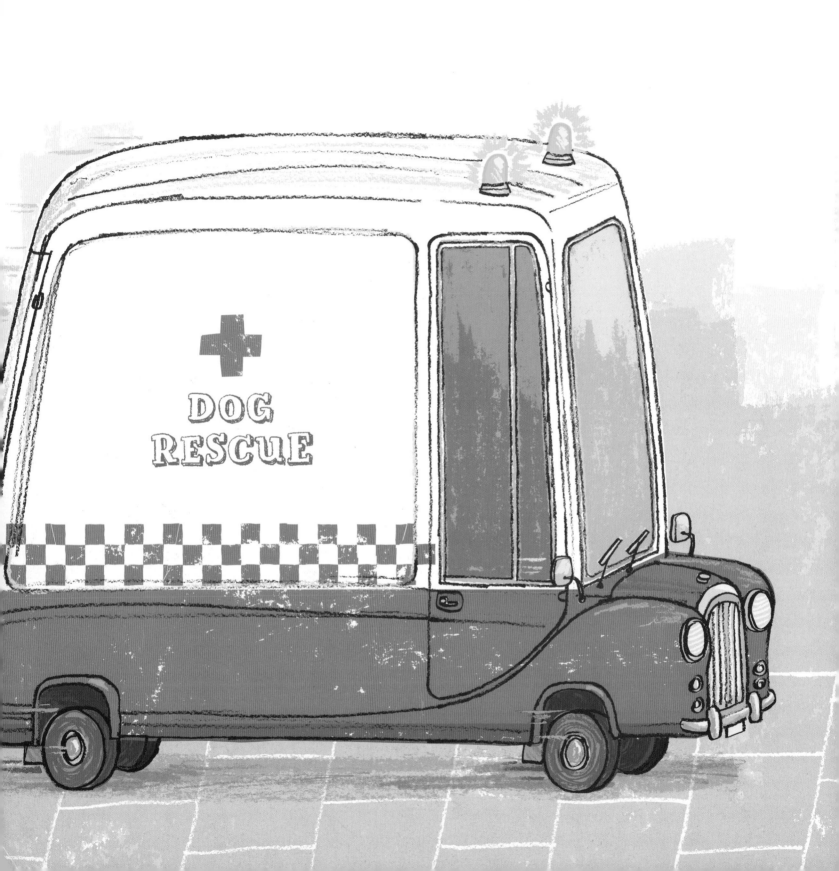

Suddenly help zoomed in . . .

. . . then vanished.

Things were getting ridiculous.

I'll just have to sort this out myself, thought Bella.

But . . .

**Sometime later,
a note appeared.**

It read . . .

Dear reader,

It would be lovely if you could kindly HELP US!

Please turn this book on its side and SHAKE...

Bella
x

1. Turn book around

2. Shake

...and SHAKE and SHAKE and SHAKE!

...and one last
little wiggle.

Thank you.

Bella x

Everybody reappeared . . .

. . . and things got back to normal.

Well, almost!

Dear reader,

Please tell this book to promise
not to be so naughty next time
you read it.

Thank you.

Bella
x

I promise to try and not be a naughty book
I promise to try and not be a naughty book
I promise to try and not be a naughty book
I promise not to be a naughty book
I promise not to be a naughty book
I promise not to be a naughty book
I promise not to be a naughty book
I promise not to be a naughty book
I promise not to be a naughty book
I promise not to be a naughty book
I promise not to be a naughty book
I promise not to be a naughty book
I promise not to be a naughty book
I promise not to be a naughty book
I promise not to be a naughty book
I promise not to be a naughty book
I promise not to be a naughty book
I promise not to be a naughty book
I promise not to be a naughty book